READY FOR A CHALLENGE

Missy Malone is running for president?" I grunt. It can't be true. Can it?

"The worst part is, nobody is running against her." Doyle wiggles the page.

My mind is racing. I'm not sure what to do. Suddenly, I have an idea. "Give me your pen."

He fumbles for it, and hands it to me. "Good thinking. Cross out her name."

"I'm not crossing out her name." Instead, I write my name right beside Never Missy's. I make sure my letters are twice the size of hers. I turn my *s* into a rattlesnake head with fangs. I make the fangs shoot venom at Never Missy's happy face *o*.

Doyle laughs. "I like it."

"You'll vote for me, won't you?"

He takes back his pen. "You have to ask?"

We do our secret handshake.

SCAB FOR ~~PRESIDENT~~
~~VICE-PRESIDENT~~
~~SECRETARY~~
TREASURER?

SECRETS OF A LAB RAT

NO GIRLS ALLOWED (DOGS OKAY)

MOM, THERE'S A DINOSAUR IN BEESON'S LAKE

SCAB FOR TREASURER?

TRUDI TRUEIT

Secrets of a Lab Rat

SCAB FOR ~~PRESIDENT~~
~~VICE-PRESIDENT~~
~~SECRETARY~~
TREASURER?

ILLUSTRATED BY **JIM PAILLOT**

ALADDIN
NEW YORK LONDON TORONTO SYDNEY

ALADDIN

An imprint of Simon & Schuster Children's Publishing Division
1230 Avenue of the Americas, New York, NY 10020

Text copyright © 2011 by Trudi Trueit
Illustrations copyright © 2011 by Jim Paillot
All rights reserved, including the right of reproduction in whole or in part in any form.
ALADDIN is a trademark of Simon & Schuster, Inc.,
and related logo is a registered trademark of Simon & Schuster, Inc.
Also available in an Aladdin hardcover edition.
For information about special discounts for bulk purchases,
please contact Simon & Schuster Special Sales at 1-866-506-1949
or business@simonandschuster.com.
The Simon & Schuster Speakers Bureau can bring authors to your live event.
For more information or to book an event contact the Simon & Schuster Speakers
Bureau at 1-866-248-3049 or visit our website at www.simonspeakers.com.
Designed by Karin Paprocki
The text of this book was set in Minister Light.
The illustrations for this book were rendered digitally.
Manufactured in the United States of America 0112 OFF
2 4 6 8 10 9 7 5 3
ISBN 978-1-4169-6113-0 (pbk)
ISBN 978-1-4169-7594-6 (hc)
ISBN 978-1-4424-2360-2 (eBook)

For Carter,

and thrill-seekers everywhere

★ ACKNOWLEDGMENTS ★

I've often said, if you long to understand the world, read a book. If you long to understand yourself, then write one. Many people have supported me on this extraordinary trek of self-discovery: my parents, who nurtured my creativity (and didn't freak out when I introduced them to my imaginary friend, Squawky); my husband, Bill, who holds my hand through all things fabulous and fearful; my agent, Rosemary Stimola, who reminds me to follow my heart no matter where it leads; and my editor, Liesa Abrams, who has granted me the greatest of all wishes—to be, freely and happily, myself. Finally, to Tanya (Tuna), Alexandra, Marilyn, Natalie, Marci, and all of my Scenic Hill Elementary friends and classmates—then and now, you inspire me.

SCAB FOR ~~PRESIDENT~~ ~~VICE-PRESIDENT~~ ~~SECRETARY~~ TREASURER?

CHAPTER

1

Missy Malone Is an Alien . . .
Pass It On

"Scab, please remove the number two pencil from your nose," says Miss Sweetandsour. "You know what to do."

I know what to do, all right. I just don't want to do it.

I am supposed to stand up, which is dumb because in two seconds I will have to sit right back down again. Miss Sweeten is giving me that squished up lemon face—the one that earned her the nickname Miss Sweetandsour. I have no choice

but to obey my teacher. I blow the pencil out of my
left nostril. There's a wet glob of tan snot on the eraser.
I get to my feet. I stand to the left of my desk and
try not to look at Missy Malone, who is standing to
the right of my desk. I snap my wrist to zing the snot
chunk in her direction. Too gooey. Won't budge.

Every Friday our teacher makes us play Fly
Around the World. It's a math flash card game. Miss
Sweetandsour goes through a stack of addition,
subtraction, multiplication, and division flash cards.
She flips one up for the champion and the challenger
to do in their heads. Whichever kid shouts out the
right answer first gets to be the champion and "fly on"

to the next challenger. The idea is to see how many kids you can beat as you move around the classroom.

I hate the game. Not because I don't like math (I do), but because I never win. That's the problem. Nobody ever wins, except Missy Malone. She flies around the world, yelling out the answers before her challengers even finish reading the cards. It's no wonder my friends and I call her Never Missy. She sits in front of me so I am usually her first victim. Never Missy has already beaten me once today and is back to whip my butt again. For her, the game is Fly Around the World. For the rest of us, it is Crash and Burn.

Never Missy smells like burned onion rings. She stares at me through brown bangs so shiny, they look wet. She smirks. Two little dimples appear on each side of her mouth. Easy target, she is thinking. She is right. I hate that she is right.

My hands are sweaty. So are my armpits. The meatballs I had for lunch are wrestling in my stomach. Miss Sweetandsour is shuffling her flash cards.

Leaning back, I look for my best friend. Doyle Ferguson is in the far front corner by the cubby rack. We're so far apart he might as well be in Antarctica. When I see him, I cross my eyes, scrunch my nose, and point to Never Missy's back. Doyle pulls his mouth all the way back with both thumbs. He sticks his tongue out and waggles it. We both think Never Missy is a space alien—and not in a good way, either. Her mustard-onion-chili breath can peel the paint off your bike. She wears tiny paper party-favor umbrellas in her hair. She never takes off her puffy, purple jacket. *Never.* We think it's because Never Missy doesn't want anybody to see the slimy green tentacles she's got hiding under there.

"Scab? Missy?" Miss Sweetandsour is ready.

I wipe my sticky hands on the sides of my jeans. This is it. This time I am going to beat Never Missy. I know, I know, I say it every Friday afternoon, but today I mean it. My heart beats faster. One teriyaki meatball leaps into my throat. The card comes up. For a second I think the meatball will too.

IS SOMEONE IN YOUR CLASS
★ AN ALIEN? ★

Does the kid clean out his/her desk every day? Aliens are neat freaks.

Does the kid always have food stuck in his/her teeth? Aliens don't use dental floss.

Does the kid have a poodle? Poodles can speak Martian, Klingon, and French.

Does the kid wear a big coat? Aliens have to hide all tentacles, tails, giant suckers, and ray guns, or the principal won't let them come to school.

If you answered yes to most of the above questions, you probably know an alien. Don't panic! Act like nothing is wrong and you probably won't get your guts sucked out through your skull.

I see white. And two black lines. It's eleven times—

"Forty-four!" shouts Never Missy.

Bug spit!

"Correct," says Miss Sweetandsour. "Four times eleven is forty-four."

I want to see the instant replay. Never Missy has to be cheating. Nobody could read the card that fast. Nobody *human*, that is.

"Excellent, Missy," says Miss Sweetandsour. She makes a mark on her notepad. "You may fly on."

Meaning, of course, that I crash and burn. See? Isn't this about as fun as getting a baby tooth yanked?

Never Missy flicks back her stringy bangs. She glances at me and says what she says to everyone she blows out of the sky with her math missiles. "Vroom, vroom, sor-reeeeee."

She doesn't sound "vroom, vroom, sorry." She sounds "vroom, vroom, happy."

"Like I care," I say, crumpling into my seat.

I don't even have the pencil back in my nose before Never Missy has crushed Cloey Zittle behind me.

"Fifty-six!" Followed by, "Vroom, vroom, sor-reeeeee."

Cloey lets out a whimper.

On and on and on Never Missy flies, "vroom-vroom-sorry"-ing her way around the room.

"Fourteen! Sixty-three! Seven!"

She's picking off kids left and right. It's enough to make you airsick. I should know. I hurled on an airplane once, and not in a barf bag either.

My twin, Isabelle, was sitting next to me. My parents had to buy her a new T-shirt. And jeans. And socks. And shoes. My sister now refuses to sit anywhere near me on a plane.

"Zero!" shouts Never Missy. Down goes my second best friend, Will Greenleaf. "Vroom, vroom, sor-reeeeee."

Some kids have their heads on their desks. Others are slumped so far down you can barely see the tops of their heads. Meggie Kornblum is— Is she crying? Aw, geez, this is ugly. Miss Sweetandsour doesn't seem to notice. Or care. She simply makes another

★ 7 ★

mark on her pad as Never Missy soars swiftly down one row and up the next.

When it's Doyle's turn, he takes his time getting up. He glances at the clock. I know what he's planning. He figures if he goes slower than a caterpillar the bell will ring first. Nice try. We still have five minutes until the end of the day—plenty of time for Never Missy to blow through another row. Doyle glances my way.

I throw my fist in the air to say *Don't give up*.

He makes a fist to reply *I won't*.

"Doyle. Missy. Ready?" asks Miss Sweetandsour.

Doyle hunches forward like he's the center facing off at the start of a hockey game. His eyes narrow. His cheeks glow. He's waiting for Miss Sweetandsour to drop the puck. I look away. I can't watch—

"Nine!"

At least it was quick—whoa! That wasn't Never Missy. Cloey slaps me between my shoulder blades. The class is starting to realize that something incredible has happened. At least, we think it has. Because Doyle is the last kid in the farthest corner of the room, nobody can get a clear look at the flash card. We rise up. We stretch our necks. Can it be true? Has my best friend done the impossible? Has Doyle Ferguson beaten the unbeatable Never Missy Malone?

Miss Sweetandsour turns to show us the card. "Incorrect," she says.

The class groans. We collapse into our chairs.

"Missy?" asks the teacher.

"Twenty-four," says Missy. Yawning, she draws her arms up into her purple sleeves.

"Correct. Seventy-two divided by three is twenty-four."

Missy makes her empty sleeves flop up and down. She turns to Doyle. "Vroom, vroom, sor-reeeeee."

Doyle's neck goes limp.

Our teacher spies the clock. "We'll have to stop here."

Everyone cheers. Miss Sweetandsour looks surprised. I am surprised that she looks surprised. HELLO! FOURTH-GRADERS DYING HERE.

Do we have to scrawl it in huge letters across the white board?

"Congratulations, Missy," says Miss Sweetandsour. "You are today's winner of Fly Around the World

SCREAM-O-METER EXPERIMENT . . . EEEEEEEEEEEK HOW LONG CAN ISABELLE SCREAM ⭐ WITHOUT TAKING A BREATH? ⭐

TEST ITEM	TIME
Salt poured in orange juice	03 seconds
Grasshopper placed on head	08 seconds
Rubber garter snake in pink unicorn purse	12 seconds
Real garter snake in pink unicorn purse	19 seconds (We have a winner!)

with—let's see—thirty-seven stops. Great job! Let's hear it for Missy."

Beth Burwell and Meggie Kornblum give up a couple of pity claps—that's when you let your right hand fall limply into your left so it barely makes a noise.

"Whoop-tee-doo," says Cloey Zittle flatly into my left ear.

"Missy, you may pick out a prize from the prize box," says Miss Sweetandsour.

I moan and let my head fall forward until it touches my desk. Will it ever be my turn to get a prize? It's been soooooo long. I've had my eye on a glow-in-the-dark white rubber rat forever. It's got a long, wiggly tail; wire whiskers; and fire-red eyes. It's perfect for hiding in my sister's sheets—for experimental purposes, of course.

Soon, Never Missy is skipping back down my row. And humming. As she slides into her chair, the back of her floppy purple hood touches my desk. I flick it off. I don't want anything of hers touching anything of mine.

"People, this floor is not as neat as it could be," announces Miss Sweetandsour. "Please patrol your area. Remember to bring in your three-dimensional nature art projects on Monday. They are due at the *beginning* of class. Also, Monday is the last day to sign up to run for a class office, so see me if you're interested. . . ." She keeps talking as she passes Doyle.

My best friend is still standing beside his desk. He hasn't moved since blurting out the wrong answer.

Never Missy is humming louder. She isn't picking up around her desk the way Miss Sweetandsour told us to do. Instead, she is drawing happy faces on her knuckles with the prize she picked out: a red gel pen with a puffball. Two wiggly eyes are glued on the puffball. They are looking at me cross-eyed. I cross my eyes back.

"Scab, up!" calls Miss Sweetandsour. I scramble out of my seat and start patrolling around my desk. I find a scrap of yellow paper, part of a maple leaf, a mangled staple— What's this? Ah, a dead potato bug. Sweet! It'll be a great addition to my art project.

Carefully, I roll the bug up in the yellow scrap of paper. I scoot across the room to the cubby rack so I can put the bug in the pocket of my backpack. Then, making sure my teacher is looking the other way, I sneak over to Doyle.

I nudge him. "You okay?"

"Uh-huh." He moves his head for the first time in two minutes. "I thought it was an eight. I was so positive it was seventy-two divided by eight—"

"Forget it," I say.

"That game stinks. I don't see why Miss Sweet-andsour makes us play it so much."

"Don't you? She's been complaining about her car a lot lately—her *old* car."

"Are you saying—?"

"Why else?"

He slaps his forehead. "Teacher torture points. How many do you think she got?"

"Today? Four hundred, at least. Maybe five hundred."

Doyle whistles through his front teeth. I can't do

★ DID YOU EVER WONDER... ★

WHY KIDS AREN'T ALLOWED IN THE FACULTY ROOM at school? Because then we'd see the Teacher Torture Board. Here's how it works. Every time a teacher makes you suffer, she gets points.

- ★ Pop quiz: 50 points
- ★ Not letting you go to the bathroom after you drank three juice boxes at lunch: 100 points
- ★ Calling or e-mailing your parents: 250 points (bonus: 150 points if she does it in front of your class)
- ★ Forcing you to play Fly Around the World with Never Missy: 500 points

At the end of the year, the teacher who gets the most points wins a car. How do I know? This year, Mrs. Dewmeyer is driving a new silver sports car. And she was *my* teacher last year.

that. But then, he has a bigger space there than I do. We watch as Miss Sweetandsour stops to talk to Never Missy. She puts her hand on a puffy, purple sleeve. Our teacher completely ignores the wads of paper littering the floor around Never Missy's desk. Miss Sweetandsour smiles. Her dark green eyes get

★ 14 ★

all soft and crinkly. Never Missy smiles back. My stomach hurts.

"I wish Miss Sweetandsour would let us do stunts," I say to myself. Doyle, Will, and I are the Daredevil Boys. We aren't afraid to climb, crawl, jump, swim, slide, or sail over most anything! I hold the world's record for flying the farthest (ten feet, nine inches) off Alec Ichikawa's Super Colossal Dirt Bike Ramp. This year, Doyle and I built the Mighty Maze in my backyard. It's the best obstacle course in town. I hold the record on that, too—22.5 seconds. If we could do at school what *I* do best, I could beat the unbeatable Never Missy. But we can't. Mrs. Zaff won't let you climb, crawl, jump, swim, slide, sail, or fly over stuff at school. She's the lunch and playground monitor. Mrs. Zaff always wears the same thing: yellow galoshes, a yellow rain coat with orange tabby cats all over it, and a plastic rain bonnet. She ties the bonnet in a big bow under her chin. The clear plastic makes her fluffy, gray hair look like a bowl of mashed potatoes. It's Mrs. Zaff's job to stop you whenever you're doing something cool, like hoisting yourself up the flagpole or spitting sunflower seeds at girls. She's always blowing her whistle at someone on the playground. Usually me. *Thweet. Thweet. Thweeeeeet.*

Doyle deflates into his desk. "I was so sure it was an eight. . . ."

"Forget it," I say, but we both know he won't.

Neither of us will. Because next Friday we'll have to play Crash and Burn all over again.

Vroom, vroom, sor-reeeeee.

2

No Spitting, Scratching, Swearing, or Pickles

I bounce the basketball. One. Two. Three times. I jut my chin out and back. I do this three times, too. I spit on the ground once to the right of my right shoe, once to the left of my left shoe, and once on the ground in front of me. I hope my sister isn't watching. Isabelle will tattle to our parents, for sure. It's her hobby—tattling on me, I mean. That, and reminding me of how brilliant she is because she got to jump ahead a grade this year. She is in the fifth grade instead of the fourth with me. My hobby is seeing how many earthworms it takes to fill up her ballet shoes. It takes nineteen per shoe, by the way. My sister has HUGE feet. Isabelle may be the smart one, but I've got more worms. (Don't worry, I always put all the earthworms back in my mom's herb garden when I am done with my experiments.)

Anyway, I'm not supposed to spit on our driveway. It is one of my mother's rules. It's a silly rule. It's not like my spit is going to eat through the concrete.

"Are you done yet?" Will's got his hands on his hips.

"Quiet." I crouch down. I lift my arms and aim for the basket. I pump the ball three times.

"I only have a half hour to play, you know."

I shake my head. It's no good. He's broken my focus. I will have to start over. I dribble the basketball three times. I jut my chin out and back. Out and back. Out and back.

"Oh, man," says Will.

"Put a lid on it or he'll never shoot," I hear Doyle say to him.

I get into aiming stance. I pump the ball three times.

✶ MY MOTHER'S RULES ✶

✶ No eating in my room.*

✶ No sticking out my tongue, especially when Aunt Judith serves dead fish with the eyes staring at me.

✶ No singing around Isabelle's Girl Scout troop, even if they request my special song, "If You're Happy and You Know It . . . Slap Your Butt."

✶ No swearing, burping, nose-picking, or spitting in public.

✶ No pretending to find beetles in the bean salad at the Happy Troll Buffet.

*If my mom is worried about the food attracting bugs, mice, and stuff . . . uh . . . too late. I already have my own ant farm, and it isn't in a fiberglass box, if you know what I mean.

"What's the point of all this hocus pocus stuff?" asks Will.

I let the ball fly. It makes a perfect arc. I smile at Will. The ball hits the backboard. I throw my arms up. "It brings good luck," I shout as we watch the ball spin around the rim three times. And bounce off.

"Usually for me." Doyle grins.

Will snags the ball. "Can we pass and shoot like normal before I have to go?"

"Sure," Doyle and I say.

Will takes the ball to the back of my driveway. He goes left then right before passing off to Doyle. My best friend dribbles a few times as he heads toward the basket. He tosses the ball to me. I run into the center, dribbling all way. At the last second, I swing the ball out to Will on my left, who gets off a beauty of a layup. *Swish!*

"Two in the hole!" shouts Doyle.

"Sweet!" I yell.

"Woof!" barks my dog, Joe. He's on the grass with his favorite toy, a piece of knotted rope. Joe is sitting up, which means he wants to play.

"In a minute, Joe," I say. I rebound and we start again at half court.

"What did you do for your 3-D nature art project?" Doyle asks me.

"I've got something in mind."

"In mind? You mean, you haven't started it yet? It's Sunday, Scab. It's due tomorrow."

I chuck the ball to him. "Thanks for the reminder, *Mom*," I say, which makes Will laugh. "It'll be easy," I explain. "I've got almost everything I need in my lab. All I have to do is put it all together." Now that I think about it, being an artist isn't that much different from being an inventor. It's all about original ideas, right? And my art project is going to be the most original thing Miss Sweetandsour has ever seen. Guaranteed!

"I hope it's not going to be like your science project last year," says Doyle, dribbling past me.

"What? My meteorite was cool."

"You mean, hot, don't you? Good thing Mrs. Dewmeyer had that fire extinguisher."

"Fire extinguisher?" asks Will. He wasn't in our class last year.

"It was no big deal," I say. "I was trying to get it to smoke like a real meteorite and it—"

"Caught fire?" gasps Will. "You started a fire at school?"

"No, no, no. There was a little smoke, that's all. Doyle, are you ever going to pass the ball?"

He leans toward Will. "It was a fire, all right. He torched Mrs. Dewmeyer's white purse. The thing looked like a giant burned marshmallow."

"Whoa!" says Will.

"And he got her world globe, too. Totally fried the Arctic Circle."

"*Whoa!*"

"Not the whole thing," I correct. "Just a little of Greenland and Canada. You can hardly tell. Canada is a big place."

"Don't forget about Iceland," says Doyle.

"What about Iceland?"

"You wiped it off the globe, Scab."

"Did not."

"Did so.

By the time we finish arguing about whether I

melted Iceland or not, it's time for Will to go. Doyle and I have homework, too, so we say good-bye. After they leave, I don't go inside right away. Instead, I play tug-of-war with Joe. I always let him win. It's fun to watch him do his victory lap around the yard with that piece of frayed rope hanging out of his mouth. "Good boy." I rub behind his ears and under his collar.

"Scab!" It's Isabelle. "Get in here."

Joe cocks his head. "Arr?"

"We could ignore her, but she'll only get louder," I tell him. "Come on, Joe, let's run." I slap my thigh. He beats me to the porch, as usual.

"Wipe his paws!" Isabelle hands me the towel we keep by the door. "Why is there peanut butter and mayo all over the kitchen counter?"

"I don't know." I pretend she is telling a joke. "Why *is* there peanut butter and mayo all over the counter, Izzy?"

"You'd better clean it up before Mom gets home from the store or I'm telling—"

SCAB'S RIPPIN' PB AND M
(AND B AND R AND BBQ)
★ SANDWICH ★

☑ your favorite kind of peanut butter (I'm a crunchy guy, myself)

☑ six banana slices

☑ twelve raisins

☑ seven barbecue potato chips

Toast two slices of bread. Spread mayo on one slice of bread and peanut butter on the other. Add bananas, potato chips, and raisins to the peanut butter side. Slap the mayo side on top. Slice crosswise to make two triangles (cut off the crusts if you hate 'em). Chow down!

"Wasn't me." I kneel down to clean Joe's paws with the towel.

"Really? Is that your story? Because we all know who eats weird food around here. It isn't Mom or Dad or me. And it sure isn't Joe."

⋆ SCAB NEWS ⋆
BY ISABELLE C. MCNALLY
(TWO-TIME CHAMPION OF THE RIVER ROCK ELEMENTARY HISTORY BEE)

⋆ 4:14 p.m. Scab spit on the driveway. Yuck!

⋆ 5:20 p.m.: Scab threw a germy sponge at me. Yuck times two!

⋆ 5:27 p.m.: Scab hasn't finished his art project. He said it was top secret, which means it isn't done. It's due tomorrow.

⋆ 5:29 p.m.: Scab took food to eat in his room, even when I told him not to.

⋆ 7:48 p.m.: Scab won't let me in his lab. Something weird is going on in there. I hear a drill.

This concludes Scab News for today. Isabelle Catherine McNally reporting.

"Woof!" barks my dog at the sound of his name.

"Power down, will you, Izzy? I'll clean it up in a minute."

Isabelle waits for me to finish toweling off Joe.

She follows me into the kitchen. She watches me scrub down the counter. "Your art project is due tomorrow."

Why does everyone think I don't know what day it is?

"What are you making?" she presses.

"It's top secret."

"You haven't taken anything of mine for it, have you?"

"Me?" I rinse out the sponge.

"Answer the question, Scab."

I pretend to think about it for a long while. "No, I haven't taken anything of yours for it. Happy?"

"Suspicious." Isabelle clicks her tongue against her teeth. "Just what are you up to, Scab McNally?"

"About four-foot-five." I toss the sponge to her. "And a half."

I grab a big jar of dill pickles from the fridge. I whistle for Joe—not that I need to. He shadows me everywhere. "We'll be in my lab, so don't bug us."

"Where are you going with that? You're not supposed to eat in your room, you know."

"I'm not."

"Then why do you need the pickles? Scab? I'm putting that in my news report to Mom and Dad!"

CHAPTER

3

Refrigerator Art

I sabelle and I ride bus number 18 to school. I am by the window. She is on the aisle. Usually, Isabelle sits several rows behind me with her friends, Laura Ling and Kendall Peters. For some reason, she has decided to park herself beside me today. I am holding the reason—a shoebox. Isabelle is trying not to look at the box, but she can't help it. My know-it-all, sneaky sister is dying to know what I have done for my art project. Naturally, I am not going to tell her.

"What's that smell?" asks Isabelle.

It's paint, glue, wood stain, spray shellac, and pickle juice. But I don't say a word.

"It's coming from your box."

"It is an old *shoe*box," I say.

My sister wrinkles her nose. "Even *your* shoes don't stink that much."

I lift my foot. "Want a fresh whiff?"

"Not again." Isabelle gags and takes off down the aisle to be with her friends.

"No standing while the bus is in motion," says Ms. Rigormortis, our driver. I am pretty sure Ms. Rigormortis is a zombie. Her pale blue skin barely stretches over her skeleton body. She rarely changes expression. I have discovered, however, that Ms. Rigormortis is pretty nice, considering she is one of the undead.

Doyle meets me as I get off the bus. His eyes go right to the box. "Can I see it?"

"Nope."

"Okay," he says quietly. I have hurt his feelings.

"It's not 'cause I don't trust you," I say, looking around for Mrs. Zaff. "I don't want anyone else to copy me. I'm going to turn it in right now. Want to help?"

STINKY SOCKS EXPERIMENT . . .
★ PEEE-EWWWW! ★

HOW MANY DAYS IN A ROW CAN A PERSON WEAR THE SAME PAIR OF SOCKS?

★ Day one–three: So far, so good. Nobody notices, though Cloey does make an odd face at me.

★ Day four: Doyle and Will hold their noses while we're playing basketball. (Try it, it isn't easy!)

★ Day ten: I ask Isabelle to sniff my feet. Her eyes roll back and she almost faints.

★ Day thirteen: Joe sniffs my feet. His eyes roll back and he *does* faint!*

★ Day nineteen: My sister holds me down while my mother pulls off my socks and throws them in the washer. Or the trash. I'm not sure which. I can't see. Isabelle was sitting on my head at the time.

★ Conclusion: You've got nineteen days before your family turns on you.

*Joe's okay

"Sure. How?"

"Clear the way. I don't want to stop for anything or anyone."

He gets in front of me. "Ready?"

"Ready."

We march up the walkway. Doyle holds the door open for me. Once we're inside, he rushes to take the lead. We walk as fast as we can without running. We don't want to get a speeding ticket from Mr. Fipps. Seriously, he does that. He comes up behind you and makes a siren sound, like he's the police pulling you over on the freeway. He even writes out a pink detention slip as if he's a cop. I'd say Mr. Fipps needs help, but he's our counselor, so technically, he *is* help. Fortunately, today Officer Fipps is nowhere in sight.

Doyle and I motor safely down the hall and into Room 242. The first bell hasn't rung so there are only a few kids in our class, which is good. Miss Sweetandsour is at her desk grading papers. She is wearing a light green dress. It reminds me of the lettuce that comes in a ball.

I set the box in front of her. "Here's my art project."

She takes off her white plastic reading glasses. "Right on time. Thank you, Scab."

My heart starts booming. I can't wait to see her look inside the box. I can't wait to see her smile at me the way she smiled at Never Missy on Friday. I can't wait to see her pretty green eyes crinkle at me. Here it comes. Miss Sweetandsour is lifting off the lid. She's peeking inside. . . .

Miss Sweetandsour's chair flies backward. It makes a loud squeak. I'm not worried. My teacher probably wants to get a better look at my work from a distance. My mom makes us go to a lot of museums so I know that's how people look at art. You're supposed to stand waaaaaay back, so you can see the whole painting or statue or whatever it is. My mom calls it "soaking up art." I don't get why a bunch of bald dollheads stacked in a pyramid is art, but I have learned not to argue with my mom about it. I can see by the way my teacher is tipping her head to the right that she is soaking up my art. Boy, she sure can soak for a long time.

Finally, Miss Sweetandsour says, "It's a . . . it's a . . ."

"Frog," I help her.

"I . . . I . . . see that."

"And a centipede, a cricket, and a potato bug."

Doyle peers into the box, which I have lined with aluminum foil. "Are they all glued to that piece of wood?"

"Yep," I say. "I tried to screw them in but that didn't work too well. See, I painted the frog bright blue and black to look like—"

"A poison dart frog!" finishes Doyle. "It looks exactly like the one in my *Amazing Amphibians of the World* book. This is great, Scab. Really great."

"Thanks." I look to Miss Sweetandsour to hear her praise, too.

Miss Sweetandsour swallows so hard, I see a lump go down the collar of her lettuce dress. "Uh, well, Scab, your frog and insects are certainly quite lifelike."

"Actually, they're deadlike."

She looks up at me. "D-dead? Are you telling me these are dead animals?"

"Uh-huh. But I didn't kill them. They were dead when I found them. Let's see—the frog died in our garden hose cart. I found the centipede under the porch, the cricket in the windowsill, and the potato bug . . ." I smile slowly. "I found that guy Friday, on the floor under my desk. Pretty lucky, huh?"

Miss Sweetandsour opens her mouth but she doesn't say anything.

"How come they're so shiny?" asks Doyle.

"Shellac spray. Three coats."

He twitches his nose. "Is that what smells so funky?"

"It's probably the combo of paint, shellac, stain, glue, and pickle juice," I say.

"Pickle juice?" Miss Sweetandsour's face is starting to blend in with her dress.

"I figure the stuff keeps pickles around forever, so why not my dead artwork, too?"

My teacher slams the top back onto the box. "Oh, my . . . uh . . . thank you, Scab. I think we should put this in the, uh . . . the staff room refrigerator. Yes,

> ## ★ AMAZING BUT DEADLY ★
>
> Poison dart frogs live in the rainforests of Central and South America. They are small—less than four inches long! They come in lots of cool patterns and colors, like red and blue, and yellow and black. But beware! Just touching the skin of a poison dart frog can kill an animal or human. Ditto for my sister's orange marmalade cookie bars. I am renaming them poison dart bars.

that's far enough away—I mean, that should keep it, uh . . . safe."

The refrigerator? I frown. Shouldn't it be displayed on the back table with the other 3-D nature sculptures? "Are you sure?" I ask. "What if someone eats it for lunch?"

But Miss Sweetandsour is already scurrying out the door. She is holding my box straight out in front of her. "Don't worry," she calls over her shoulder.

"Great job." Doyle punches me. "It's way better than Lewis's dumb old piggy bank or my crummy birdhouse," he mutters. I follow Doyle's gaze to the back table.

Sometimes, I could smack myself for not paying attention. "Hey, is that your birdhouse? Nice work."

He fiddles with some papers on Miss Sweetand-sour's desk. "Nah. Not compared to your dead art."

"Sure it is," I say, but the truth is, Doyle's birdhouse looks like a hurricane tore through it. The roof is tipped steeply to one side. The perch is hanging by a thread of glue. The crooked walls are decorated with birdseed, except there are several bare spots. A trail of seed stretches out the door of our classroom. Something tells me I could follow it all the way to Doyle's bike clamped onto the bike rack.

"No way!" shouts Doyle. "No WAY!"

"Okay, okay," I say. "Maybe I would have used a little more glue on the seed—"

> ★ **SCAB'S TIP #29** ★
>
> YOU CAN FIND THE BEST dead insects under your deck, under your porch, and under my sister's pillow. (Shhh—she hasn't found the dead stag beetle I left there yet!)

"Look at this, Scab! Just look." He is pulling me around our teacher's desk. He waves a sheet of paper in front of my nose. "Look!"

"I would if you'd hold still!" I grab his wrist. Doyle's holding the sign-up sheet for class officers. At the top, Miss Sweetandsour has written the word, PRESIDENT. Under that, I see the name—oh no! Only one person in the world turns the *o* in her name into a happy face.

"Missy Malone is running for president?" I grunt. It can't be true. Can it?

"The worst part is, nobody is running against her." Doyle wiggles the page.

"Stay calm," I say, seeing fear in his eyes. "We have all day. Maybe someone else will sign up."

"Yeah, maybe." He grabs my arm. "But what if nobody does? What then?"

I shiver. I don't want to think about that.

"She'll make us wear purple coats," says Doyle. "And do face painting. I hate face painting. She'll make us play Fly Around the World every single day.

I can't do it, Scab. Not every day." He crumples up the sign-up sheet. "Let's hide this in my desk. Wait! Let's hide it in your desk. Yeah. Your desk is so messy, Miss Sweetandsour would *never* find it there."

"It's a piece of paper, Doyle. Miss Sweetandsour will think she's lost it. She'll just make up a new list."

"So what do we do? The bell's going to ring, Scab. What do we *do*?"

My mind is racing. I'm not sure what to do.

DAREDEVIL BOYS SECRET ⋆ HANDSHAKE ⋆

⋆ Step One: Clasp thumbs

⋆ Step Two: Wiggle fingers

⋆ Step Three: Slap palms

⋆ Step Four: Knock knuckles

⋆ Step Five: Bang your chest with your fist

⋆ Step Six: Burp 'em if you got 'em

Suddenly, I have an idea. "Give me your pen."

He fumbles for it, and hands it to me. "Good thinking. Cross out her name."

"I'm not crossing out her name." Instead, I write my name right beside Never Missy's. I make sure my letters are twice the size of hers. I turn my *s* into a rattlesnake head with fangs. I make the fangs shoot venom at Never Missy's happy face *o*.

Doyle laughs. "I like it."

"You'll vote for me, won't you?"

He takes back his pen. "You have to ask?"

We do our secret handshake.

"You'll win, for sure," says Doyle. "Everybody hates Fly Around the World."

That is what I am counting on.

A few minutes later, Never Missy shuffles into the room. As usual, she is wearing her purple coat buttoned up to the neck to hide her slimy green tentacles. She's got two little yellow polka-dotted paper umbrellas in her hair. Alien antennae, no doubt. I am sitting quietly at my desk. I fold my hands. I place my feet flat on the floor, just how Miss Sweetandsour likes it. From now until the election I am going to be the perfect student. No burping. No snot flicking. No armpit noises. No fun at all. But it's for a good cause.

Never Missy flicks her brown bangs off her face. She smirks at me. Two dimples appear.

I nod. I hide my grin, but it's hard.

Never Missy has no idea that she is about to lose. I like that she has no idea. I like it a lot.

CHAPTER

4

Scab for Prez

Doyle and I have been friends since we met in the summer before second grade. He gave me my nickname. (My real name is Salvatore—talk about a disaster!) I got 148 mosquito bites at camp that year, which ended up being 148 red, itchy, globby, nubby, crusty scabs. Ta-da! Thinking up names isn't the only thing Doyle is good at. He can bounce a mini soccer ball from knee to knee fifteen times without dropping it. He can carve an exact replica of Principal Huckabee's head out of the cornbread stuffing they serve in the cafeteria. He can burp "Twinkle, Twinkle, Little Star" the whole way through without taking a breath. But, no matter how hard he tries, there is one thing Doyle Ferguson has never been able to do. My best friend cannot keep a secret.

By the time the tardy bell rings, the whole class knows I am running against Never Missy for president. Miss Sweetandsour is taking roll when Never Missy whips around. I jump back in my seat, sure a slimy tentacle is going to shoot out from under her purple coat, grab me by the neck, and squeeze me until my eyeballs pop out.

"I hear you want to be president," she says, lifting her chin.

I don't see any tentacles, so I relax. A little.

"You hear right," I say, still watching the buttons on her coat. If they even start to bulge . . .

"Why?"

I tip my head. "Why what?"

"Why do you want to be president?"

I fold my arms. "Why do you?"

"I asked you first."

"I asked you last."

★ 44 ★

TOP SECRET:
SCAB'S SUREFIRE TIPS FOR WINNING
★ A STARING CONTEST ★

★ Before the contest starts, close your eyes for one minute to get them good and watery.

★ If your eyes start to feel dry, force yourself to open them wider. This will make your eyes water so you won't have to blink.

★ Try my trick move: yawn. Yawning is contagious. When you yawn, your opponent will yawn too, and accidentally blink. Hooray! You win!

Dark gray eyes glare at me. I glare back. Neither of us wants to be the first to look away. Or to blink. Before I know it we are smack in the middle of a stare down.

Never Missy leans toward me. I don't budge. She doesn't scare me. Well, maybe those tentacles do.

"Give up, Scab."

"You give up."

"You're going to lose." Why do I get the feeling she is not talking about our stare down?

"I can do this all day," I growl. "My eyeballs could shrivel up and roll right out of their sockets and I wouldn't blink."

"Your eyeballs could roll under my desk and I could squish them with my boots and *I* wouldn't blink," she says.

"You could squish my eyeballs, trip on their slimy goo, and slide right out the door and I wouldn't blink," I say.

"Are you giving up?" she says, snarling.

I want to. Never Missy's onion-ring breath is frying off my eyebrows. But I won't. "Are you giving up?"

"I asked you first."

"I asked you last."

Thirty seconds pass. It feels like thirty minutes. Never Missy narrows her eyes. She is about to blink. I know it. At last, I am going to beat her. I open my eyes wider.

"Scab?"

I look up at Miss Sweetandsour. And my eyelids close.

Agggggghhhh!

Giggling, Never Missy swings away from me. One antenna—I mean, umbrella—falls out of her hair.

"Later," I growl.

My teacher kneels beside my desk. "Scab, did you sign up to run for class president?"

"Yes."

"Oh. Oh!" She laughs nervously. "I thought it might be Lewis playing a joke—"

BOYS VS. GIRLS

AN ORIGINAL POEM
★ BY SALVATORE W. MCNALLY ★

Girls like yellow polka dots.

Boys like giant, steel robots.

Girls like spinkled cupcakes.

Boys like chasing garter snakes.

Girls like glitter in their hair.

Boys like dirty underwear.

Girls like poems that rhyme.

Boys don't!

"No. I signed up."

"Oh." Miss Sweetandsour stands up. She wipes her hands on the front of her lettuce dress. "Okay, then. Okay then. Good. Good." She walks away.

My teacher always repeats herself when she's surprised. I guess she didn't expect anyone to run against her favorite student. Surprise!

Never Missy is humming again. She is drawing

a happy face on her wrist. I draw a rattlesnake on mine.

By first recess, Doyle has taped a sign to his desk. It reads: VOTE FOR SCAB! Soon, he's making signs for Will and me, too. With ten minutes left in the day, Miss Sweetandsour holds up her hand. After a few seconds, she bends her thumb into her palm. Then she tucks her pinky under her thumb.

"Shut up!" shrieks Cloey. If our teacher gets to zero, we'll have to stay in a whole minute from first recess tomorrow. "SHUT UP!" Cloey's second scream rattles my head. The girl has enormous lung power. But it works. We quiet down.

"Thank you," says Miss Sweetandsour. "Before you go, I want to tell you how the election will work. Each candidate may make small signs for students to place on

the front of their desks, and one big sign for the back bulletin board. On Thursday afternoon, each candidate will be given thirty seconds to make a speech, if he or she wants to. Then we'll vote by secret ballot. I'll count the ballots and announce the winners—yes, Meggie? You have a question?"

"Can we hand out candy and stuff?"

"No giveaways," Miss Sweetandsour says firmly. "The point isn't to buy votes, but to earn them. Instead of giving things away, what if you told students about some of the goals you'd like to accomplish if you're elected?"

"My goal is to give away twelve boxes of red licorice," grumbles Meggie.

"Are you ready to find out who the candidates are?" asks our teacher.

We all shout, "Yes!"

Lewis Pigford does a drumroll on his desk with a couple of chewed-up pencils. That's why his two front teeth jut out to the sides—too much pencil chomping.

Miss Sweetandsour clears her throat. "For secretary, we have Alec Ichikawa and Beth Burwell."

We all clap.

"For vice president, it's Carlton Cho and Meggie Kornblum."

We clap again.

"For president, your candidates are Missy Malone and Scab McNally."

More applause. Will and Doyle really whoop it up for me. I pump my fist in the air. Never Missy hops to her feet and bows. Show-off.

"And for treasurer . . ." Our teacher sighs and waves a piece of paper. "Well, we don't have anyone running for that spot, so if you're interested, please see me."

Behind me, Cloey mutters, "I don't think so."

I turn. "Why not?"

"I was treasurer last year in Mr. Woolwine's class. It's the worst job ever. When we order from the book clubs, you have to keep track of the orders. When we go on a field trip, you have to collect permission slips. When we do the PTA bake sale, you have to help count all the money afterward. It's a ton of work and nobody appreciates you." She pulls her light blue sweater off the back of her chair, and slips her arms into it. "You'd have to be crazy to want that job."

I nod. I'm not crazy. Nope. I'm going to be president.

Yep. Scab McNally, Class President.

Wait until my smart times ten sister hears about this.

CHAPTER
5

Hot Dog, Cool Treat

D on't be a crab, vote for Scab."

"Uh-huh."

"Don't dillydally, vote McNally."

"Uh-huh."

It's Tuesday afternoon, and Doyle, Joe, and I are in my lab. Doyle is working on my election signs. I am scribbling in my inventor's notebook. We are waiting for my dog treats to freeze. Pup-sicles are my new invention. They are pretty simple, really—cubes of ice cream with bits of Joe's favorite foods frozen inside. On my first try, the scrambled eggs turned to rubber. On my second try, the popcorn turned to mush-corn. This is my third batch, and

I think I've got the right combo of ingredients this time.

"How about 'Vote Scab for Prez, Because I Says.'"

"Uh-huh."

"Scab, you're not listening. *Scab?*"

"I'm listening." Sort of.

★ JOE'S FRUITY PUP-SICLES ★

★ Two cups of melted strawberry ice cream

★ One can of fruit cocktail (pour the juice out)

★ Three Peanut Butter & Apple Snausages (cut into small pieces)

★ Three tartar control dog biscuits (crush 'em up)

★ Five peanuts (crush these, too)

Drop a bit of fruit cocktail, Snausages, and dog biscuit into each cube of the ice cube tray. Fill each cube to the top with melted ice cream. Sprinkle with crushed peanuts. Place ice cube tray in freezer. Once the pup-sicles are frozen, pop out one or two for your dog to enjoy!

"I'm trying to come up with stuff for your signs, and you don't even care."

"I care."

"You don't act like it."

"I'm going to win. You said so yourself."

"Yeah, but you should still stick some signs up. Never Missy's got hers all over the place."

"She does?"

"Didn't you see them on everybody's desks?"

I shrug. I can't remember. "Everybody hates Fly Around the World. They'll all vote for me, you even said so yourself."

Ting! The egg timer goes off.

Doyle and I look at each other. "Pup-sicles!"

"Woof!" barks Joe.

With Doyle in the lead and Joe bringing up the rear, we charge down the stairs. I round the corner into the kitchen and bounce off of Doyle, who has stopped short. Joe runs into me.

Wuh-oh. The blue ice cube tray is sitting on the counter. One of the squares is empty.

"So that's when Kayla told Katie that Kirsten isn't going to Kami's party . . ." My sister strolls into the kitchen. She's got the cordless phone in one hand and a pink pup-sicle wrapped in a paper towel in the other. "After everything Kami did to get Kirsten onto the soccer team when she could hardly dribble the ball . . ."

"Izzy?"

"Shush. I'm on the phone."

I point to her hand. "You shouldn't—"

"Hold on a minute, Kendall. You-know-who is bothering me."

I try again. "Isabelle, you really don't want to be—"

"I know, I know, Scab, I took one of your precious ice cream treats. I should have asked first. But you made plenty, and there's no reason why you can't share."

"If you'd listen for a—"

"You know, you can be pretty selfish sometimes, Scab. It's one of your worst faults. I should probably put that in my next news report to Mom and Dad. So what do you say?" She waves the pink ice cube at me.

"I am sorry," I say politely, trying to keep the sarcasm out of my voice. "Please, Isabelle, have as many treats as you want."

"Now was that so hard?"

"No," I say, holding in a grin.

Isabelle takes a lick of pup-sicle. "Peanuts. Yum."

Doyle lets loose with a good snort. I still don't crack a smile.

"I'm back, Kendall," Isabelle says into the phone. "Where were we? . . . Uh-huh . . . uh-huh . . ." My sister takes another lick of pup-sicle. Then another.

I see Snausages.

I let a snicker escape.

> ⭐ **SCAB'S TIP #8** ⭐
>
> Never argue with a know-it-all, superspy, tattletale sister who has the combination to your top-secret safe.

Then a chuckle. Pretty soon, Doyle and I are laughing so hard we can barely stand up.

"Quiet, you two," snaps my sister. She paces to the corner of the kitchen.

My stomach is killing me. Tears are streaming down my best friend's face.

We watch Isabelle walk and talk and lick. Lick and talk and walk. "You would think Kirsten would be a little more grateful . . . uh-huh . . . uh-huh . . ."

Doyle and I are, finally, getting a grip on ourselves when it happens.

Crunch!

Dog biscuit.

"Arrooo?" Joe tips his head. Poor puppy. He can't figure out why Isabelle is eating his food. Howling, Doyle and I collapse onto the floor.

"Okay, call me—no, wait—have Kayla tell Katie to call me when she hears from Kami, okay?" Shooting me a nasty glare, Isabelle snatches another pink ice cube from the tray. She leans down to me, 'cause I am still rolling on the floor. "You know," she says, "for the first time in your life you might have actually come up with a decent invention— What?" Back to the

phone. "Oh, yeah, Kirstin is pretty clueless, isn't she? She thinks she knows everything about everyone, but half the time she has no idea what's going on . . ." My sister strolls out of the kitchen, licking the peanuts off her fresh pup-sicle.

Doyle and I start laughing all over again.

CHAPTER

6

Rats!

Where's the big sign Doyle made for you?"

"I forgot it."

My sister glares at me. "What about Doyle's desk signs?"

"Uh . . . forgot."

"Have you written your speech yet?"

"It's all here." I tap the side of my head.

"Sounds hollow to me." Isabelle looks out the bus window as we pull into the parking lot of River Rock Elementary. "How do you expect to win the election, Scab, if you don't try?"

"I'll win."

"You seem awfully confident."

"I am."

She gives me the once-over with that X-ray stare of hers. "What are you up to? And don't you dare say four-foot-five-and-a-half."

"Nothing." I hold up both hands. "Honestly."

"I hope you know you can't be this lazy after the election."

"*After* the election?" I don't see what that has to do with anything.

"The class president has a lot of responsibilities, you know. You've got to help with the PTA fundraisers, like the plant and cookie sales. You've got to be involved in the Honor Society dinner, the talent show, and Grandparents Day. Oh, and of course, there are student council meetings every Monday and Wednesday during first recess—"

"Recess?" I bolt up. Nobody said anything about having to give up recess. I play basketball with Doyle and Will every first recess. I am not about to chuck that for some dumb meeting where we argue about

SCAB'S QUESTION OF THE DAY: WHAT'S IN THE CHEF'S SPECIAL SALAD DRESSING?

WHAT THE COOKS SAY IS IN IT	WHAT THE KIDS KNOW IS IN IT
blue cheese	blue toe cheese
whipped mayonnaise	whipped maggots
vinegar	Mr. Velasko's nose hair (it's so long you can braid it!)
fresh parsley from the market	dead dandelions from the courtyard
chopped chives	chickenpox scabs

what Mrs. Chadwick and the cafeteria cooks put in the chef's Special Salad Dressing. No thanks!

As the bus comes to a stop, Isabelle gathers up

her stuff. "What did you think being president was going to be like?"

What's to think about? I want to beat Never Missy. That's all. Girls make everything so complicated. Isabelle is trying to scare me with all this talk about responsibilities. She ought to know I don't scare easily.

"Your teeth look nice," I say to my sister.

"Huh?"

"Nice and white. Tartar free."

"Ooooo-kay."

"You have a shiny coat, too."

She looks down at her navy jacket. "What are you blabbering about?"

I give her the only hint I can. "Woof."

"Boys are such a waste of oxygen."

"Have a nice day," Ms. Rigormortis says blandly as we get off the bus. "Have a nice day."

"You too," I say with a wave.

When I step onto the curb, Doyle is there. He

looks at my empty hands. "Where are the signs I made yesterday?"

"Doesn't know," Isabelle shoots over her shoulder, hurrying away.

"I forgot them," I say. "Sorry."

"But I worked on those all afternoon!"

"I know. Sorry."

"I could have called to remind you this morning, but you said you'd remember to bring them. You said I didn't have to worry about it and that you'd pack everything up and—"

"I know what I said. Quit dogging me about the signs, will you?" It comes out sounding angrier than I meant for it to. We turn into Room 242. Suddenly, I am surrounded by a purple fog. I can't see. I can't breathe. I throw a punch. *Thump*. My knuckles bounce!

"Hey, watch my balloons," says Never Missy.

"No fair," Doyle pipes up. "Teacher said we couldn't do giveaways."

"Yes, fair. It's not a giveaway. They're decorations for my signs, see?" We watch her tape a small purple

balloon to the front of a sign that reads, I'M FOR
MAL☺NE! I fake barf into Miss Sweetandsour's trash
can with the yellow tulips on it. Doyle laughs.

"Who wants a balloon?" calls Missy.

I hiss into Doyle's ear. "None of the guys are going to—"

"I do!"

When we see who comes over, our jaws drop.

"WILL!" Doyle and I shout.

"I want a balloon. Is that a crime?"

"Yes!"

We spin him and make him spit swear right then and there that he is going to vote for me.

"I was going to anyway," he mumbles. "Geez!"

When I look around, I see that I'M FOR MAL☺NE signs are everywhere. Even some of the guys—Henry, Lewis, and Juan—have *her* signs on their desks. What is going on here? I mean, she's a girl. And an alien. And a Fly Around the World pain-in-the-rump show-off. And a GIRL!

After she takes roll, Miss Sweetandsour tells us to open our science books. She starts reviewing the chapter on the water cycle. I cannot get over what is happening in my class. I was so certain everyone hated Fly Around the World as much as I did. I was so

STUFF THAT SHOULD BE
★ OUTLAWED AT SCHOOL ★

★ Pop quizzes

★ Making snowflakes (Mine always fall apart!)

★ The two words we most hate to find at the top of our papers: "See me"

★ Sporks (the plastic fork/spoon thing they make you eat with in the cafeteria)

★ Substitutes who can't pronounce anybody's name right

certain the election was going to be a snap. But now, seeing wall-to-wall purple, I am no longer certain of anything.

Cloey is flicking her fingers against my back. "Take out a piece of paper."

"What?"

"Plug your brain back in, will you? Chapter quiz."

Bug spit!

Miss Sweetandsour tells us to number our pages

to fifteen. She begins asking questions about the water cycle. How much of the Earth's surface is covered by water? How much water does your body need each day? What is the freezing point of water? I don't know. I can't remember. And thirty-two degrees Fahrenheit. (I am a scientist, after all.) When we're done with the quiz, we swap papers. I trade with Henry Mapanoo. He gets thirteen right. That's a B+. I get nine right. That's a D.

We hand our papers forward. "Did anyone answer all of the questions correctly?" asks Miss Sweetand-sour.

Never Missy's purple arm shoots up. It's official. This girl is *not* human.

"Wonderful," oozes Miss Sweetandsour. "Missy, Juan, Trina, and Carlton, you may each come up and pick out something from the prize box."

Whoa, whoa, whoa!

Nobody said anything about this being a prize quiz. No fair! I kick the leg of my desk. If only I'd paid attention. I could be up there right now snagging my glow-in-the-dark rat. I kick my desk again. Ouch. I watch Miss Sweetandsour take the top off the red plastic storage bin marked PRIZE BOX. I can't look. I spin in my seat. "Hey, Cloey?"

She is brushing her hair. Her bangs make a wavy curtain in front of her face. "Uh-huh?"

"You're voting for me, aren't you?"

"Maybe."

"Maybe? Don't you hate Fly Around the World as much as I do?"

She runs a brush through her hair curtain. "Sure, but we're talking class president here, Scab."

"So?"

She parts her hair on the left side, pulling the biggest chunk over to clip on the right. "It's like what Miss Sweetandsour told Meggie." She sees the confusion on my face. "You should try to earn our votes."

"How do I—?"

"Weren't you listening? What are your goals? What will you do if you're elected?"

I puff out my chest. "I'll get rid of Fly Around the World."

She clicks her tongue. "That's it?"

"Isn't that enough?"

"It's just a game, Scab."

I almost fall out of my chair. A game? A *game*? Earth to Cloey! How could she say that? It's about Never Missy *always* winning and the rest of us *always* losing! It's about Miss Sweetandsour treating Never Missy better than everyone else. It's about right and wrong. Fair and unfair. Good and evil. Fly Around the World is a lot of things, but it is *not* just a game.

"You should do a handout," says Cloey. "You know, like Missy's."

I stiffen. "Missy's?"

"Didn't you get one?"

"No."

"I think I've got one here in my desk. Yeah, here it is—see how she's written out her goals? She says what she wants to do if we elect her." Cloey shoves a light purple piece of paper at me, but I push it away. I don't want to see anything of *hers*.

On the back bulletin board, white block letters almost jump off the large purple poster: DON'T MISS-Y OUT ☺N THE BEST: VOTE MISSY MAL☺NE FOR CLASS PRESIDENT. I whirl around in my seat. If I see one more happy face o or purple balloon I will explode. It would be worth it to spew my blood, guts, and brains all over Never Missy's desk. Not that Miss Sweetandsour would make her clean me up. She never makes her straighten up around her desk. I look across the room for Doyle, but there are too many balloons in the way. I throw my pen at the one on Lewis's desk to try to pop it. The pen just bounces off the chubby balloon and rolls away.

Never Missy is skipping down our row. She is smiling. She's swinging—no! NO! She's dangling a white, glow-in-the-dark, rubber rat—*my* glow-in-the-dark, rubber rat!

Never Missy slides into her chair. She starts humming.

It takes all of my energy not to scream *That's mine! You stole MY rat.* The only thing that stops me is that I know that's what she wants me to do. She wants me to get mad. She did this on purpose. Never Missy probably doesn't even want the rat. She'll probably draw a happy face on it with her red puffball pen and dress it up in a little purple coat. I fling her hood off the edge of my desk. So Cloey wants to know what I stand for, huh? She wants to know my goals, huh?

Here's one: Never Missy has won for the last time. And that's more than a goal. That's a promise.

7

Ka-boom?

I'll snag the b-ball," says Doyle. Our class is lining up for first recess. "You guys save the good court—"

I wave him off. "I'm calling an emergency meeting." I karate chop a purple balloon on Juan's desk. It comes loose. I kick it away. Don't any of these stupid things pop?

"Okay!" Doyle bounces his head as if to say, "Finally."

Miss Sweetandsour must be feeling more sweet than sour today, because when I ask her if Doyle, Will, and I can stay in during recess to work on my campaign signs she says yes. After everybody leaves, our teacher shuts us in the classroom, locks the door from the hall, and goes to check her score on the Teacher Torture Board. Will and I start churning out desk signs, while Doyle tackles the big banner for the back bulletin board.

He rolls out a long piece of tan butcher paper. "Never Missy's got a good head start on you, Scab,

SCAB'S TOP SECRET
✳ PERSONAL INFO ✳

✳ I didn't give up blanky wanky (my baby blanket) until I was eight.

✳ Sometimes, I wear my pajamas with the feet attached. They have sheep on them. I feel stupid. It has to be really cold out.

✳ I still sleep with Howard, the stuffed musical rabbit Grandma Lu gave me when I was two. You got a problem with that?

Spit swear, please, that all the above information will be kept confidential. Thank you.

but we'll turn it around. What do you want your sign to say?"

"Something funny."

"And short," adds Will.

"Funny and short," murmurs Doyle. As he thinks, my best friend chews on his thumbnail, or what's left of it. I suspect Doyle still sucks his thumb. I don't tease him about it, though. We all have stuff to deal with.

"How about 'Vote Scab McNally'?" asks Doyle.

"Short," says Will. "Not funny."

Doyle munches on his thumbnail some more. "How about this one: 'We Won't Have to Play Fly Around the World when Scab's Class President.'"

"Not short," I say. "And not funny."

More thumbnail biting then, suddenly, Doyle throws his arms into the air. "I've got it. 'Pick Scab.' Get it? *Pick* Scab."

We get it. We laugh. We like it. Short *and* funny.

Will and I each make six desk signs. They're not as nice as Never Missy's fancy poster board signs.

My writing slants too much. The letters are bunched together because I ran out of room. Will spelled my name wrong on his signs. They read MCNAILY FOR PREZ. Plus, we don't have any decorations. No balloons. No glitter. No stickers.

"What's the matter?" asks Doyle. He knows me from the bones out.

"My signs stink."

Doyle looks them over. "That one's not so bad."

I hold my nose. "They stink. I wish I had . . . I need . . ."

"What?"

"I don't know . . . more."

"More signs?"

"No, I mean . . . I mean . . ." I pull my hair straight up in the air. I don't know what I mean. But I am starting to freak out.

"You could write out what you'll do if you're elected president, like Never Missy did," says Doyle. "Do you want to see what she—"

"No! I don't want to do a crummy handout."

Will looks up from his desk. He's got a big streak of blue ink on his chin. "What, then?"

"I'm not sure. This election is boring. I want to have fun. And I want to do something I'm good at doing." An idea is beginning to form in my brain.

"I want to do something I'm good at doing and something Never Missy isn't good at doing." Yes, I'm definitely getting an idea!

"You mean something daring?" Doyle grins. He is reading my mind, as usual. I nod.

"Something so cool that when kids see it they'll *have* to vote for you?" Will's got it now.

Together, we shout, "Stunt!"

We are congratulating ourselves when Doyle stops to ask, "What kind of stunt?"

I clasp my hands on top of my head and walk around the room. This is how I do my best thinking.

"You've got to do it at school where everyone can watch it," says Will.

I agree. And keep walking.

"You'll have to be careful not to get Zaffed," Doyle reminds us. He's talking about Mrs. Zaff, the lunch and playground monitor. Just yesterday, she was blowing her whistle at me.

Thweet. Thweet. Thweeeeeet.

"Scab McNally! What in the world are you doing?"

Her plastic-covered mashed-potato head charged my way. She was wearing her bright yellow raincoat with the orange tabby cats, even though it was a sunny day.

"Uh . . . cleaning my rocks? This one's got a slug on it."

"Not in the water fountain. Get those rocks out of there. Pronto."

"Okay."

"Break it up." She swung her cat umbrella to get rid of the kids who'd come over to see what was going on. *Thweet. Thweet. Thweeeeeet.*

Maybe that should be one of my campaign promises. I, Scab McNally, promise to drop Mrs. Zaff's whistle in the toilet. *Flush. Flush. Whooooosh.*

"Scab." Will is pointing to the door.

Isabelle's face is smooshed up against the long, skinny window.

What is *she* doing here? Of course! The second I didn't show up on the playground for recess, my sister, Superspy, began tracking me with her supersister radar. Recess is half over. What took her so long?

"You've got my lunch," Isabelle says when I open the door. "I've got yours."

"How do you know?"

"I know." She rolls her eyes. "My whole class knows." She opens the bag.

I take a whiff. "Ah, bologna, egg, marshmallow, and ketchup on rye."

"Ew. Take it, will you, before I throw up?"

"I'll get yours."

While I go to the cubby rack, Superspy strolls around the room. "Nice sign, Doyle," she says flatly. "*Pick Scab*. Real mature."

"Thanks," he says with pride.

I hand Isabelle her lunch. "Thank goodness you have it. I didn't bring any money today, and no way was I going to eat that cootie sandwich of yours. Not that it even compares to that nasty wrap-thingy you made yesterday—"

"You didn't even try it."

"Salami, applesauce, and sour cream-and-onion potato chips in a tortilla? I don't think so."

"You forgot the blueberry jelly beans."

She gags. "I don't know how you do it. One of these days your stomach is going to explode. Kaboom!"

"Will not. My stomach's made of iron. It's tough and strong. It can handle anyth—" I freeze.

That's it! An amazing, one-of-a-kind stunt that will get everyone to vote for me. It's perfect!

"Scab?" I hear Doyle calling me, but my brain is too busy to answer. My hands are on the top of my head again. I begin circling Miss Sweetandsour's desk. Slowly at first, then faster and faster and faster.

Will starts to say, "Hey, Scab, maybe you could—"

"Ssshhh," says Doyle. "He's getting an idea. It must be for his stunt."

"A stunt?" Isabelle gulps. "You mean a daredevil stunt?"

"Uh-huh," answers Doyle.

"Here?"

"Uh-huh."

Will's eyebrows go up. He slaps his thigh. "Oh, boy!"

Isabelle's eyebrows go down. She slaps her cheeks and sighs. "Oh, boy."

I barely hear her. I am working out the details of the most difficult stunt I have ever attempted. It will be the most incredible stunt in the history of River Rock Elementary. And the best part is, Never Missy won't be able to stop me. Or beat me.

8

The Human Vacuum

Doyle tapes a sign to the front of my chest. Will slaps another one on my back. The three of us walk single file into the cafeteria. I'm in the middle. At River Rock Elementary, each class is assigned a row of tables for lunch. Our class is in the first row so it doesn't take long for kids to read my signs. Coming and going, I say the same thing:

SCAB MCNALLY THE HUMAN VACCUUM

YOU BRING IT HE'LL EAT IT

VOTE SCAB

"Hey, Scab!" shouts Henry Mapanoo. "Will you
eat salt?"

"Sure, that's easy," I say with a snort.

"How about a lemon?" asks Juan.

"I won't even make a face."

"What about sardines?" cries Beth.

"I love 'em." That one is true.

"Artichokes?"

"Sauerkraut?"

"Scorpion tails?"

"Goat cheese?"

"Yep, yep, yep, and yep," I call. "I'll eat anything!"
Scorpion tails?

"Seriously? Anything?" asks Lewis Pigford. "Even dirt?"

"Dirt?" shouts Alec Ichikawa. "Hey, everybody, Scab's going to eat dirt!"

"No!" says Doyle, waving his arms. "Not dirt. Will, you'd better fix that."

Will crosses out the first IT and writes FOOD on my signs.

I am glad. I'm not crazy about chowing down on dirt, worms, or lint. Sure, I'll eat them, but I'd rather not if I don't have to. . . .

"I've got the sign-up sheet," Doyle calls out. "Write down what you are going to bring tomorrow. The Human Vacuum promises to eat one bite of each thing. The line starts here— Hey, quit pushing. Take it easy. Everybody will get their turn."

My best friend is soon swallowed up by the crowd. Sweet! This is going to be my best stunt ever.

Never Missy is beside me. She is twirling a paper umbrella above her left ear. "Miss Sweetandsour said we couldn't do any giveaways. No fair."

"Yes, fair," I shoot back. "I am not giving anything away. Kids are bringing stuff to *me*. There's no rule against that."

Her face red, Never Missy stomps away.

I've never felt so good. Or so powerful.

"Scab, will you eat fruitcake?" shouts Carlton Cho. "It's been in our pantry for, like, ten years."

"Bring it!"

Isabelle is charging toward me, wildly shaking her carton of chocolate milk. "Scab McNally, you take those signs off right now. I thought you were kidding with this whole human vacuum thing."

She really ought to know better. "No such luck," I say. "I'm doing the stunt."

"You're nuts," says Isabelle. "Completely nuts."

"Yeah, I'll eat any kind of nuts," I say loudly for

everyone around us to hear. To her, I hiss, "Go away, Izzy. You'll ruin everything."

"You think I'm ruining it *now*?"

Bug spit! She is going to tattle.

"Come on, Isabelle, it's only for a few votes."

"Of all the stupid stunts you've done in your lifetime, Scab, this tops it. You're going to get sick. Or worse."

"I can do this. What about all the crazy recipes I've invented on my own, like peanut butter–root beer floats and salami-applesauce wraps?"

"That doesn't mean—"

"My stomach can take it. You said so."

"What I *said* was that your stomach was going to explode."

"Trust me, Isabelle, I can eat anything."

"Anything?" says Lewis.

"I'm *not* eating dirt, Lewis!" I shout. I move my sister to the end of the row. "Please, Isabelle, don't tattle. This is my chance to win the election."

★ SCAB NEWS ★
BY ISABELLE C. MCNALLY
(FIRST RUNNER-UP,
GIRL SCOUTS REGIONAL POETRY CONTEST)

* 8:25 a.m.: Scab forgot his campaign signs at home. He hasn't written anything for his speech tomorrow either.

* 9:38 a.m.: Scab took my lunch, but I got mine back at first recess. Mom, please write his name on his lunch sack in GIGANTIC letters so this does not happen again.

* 12:14 p.m.: I saw Scab at lunch. HINT: I can't tell you if he's up to something, but you might want to ask him what he's having for *his* lunch tomorrow.

* 1:54 p.m.: Laura told me she saw Scab turning all of the books upside down in the library display case!

* 4:37 p.m.: Scab threw me out of his lab (how rude!) and locked the door.

* 6:07 p.m.: Scab still hasn't put the jar of pickles back yet in the refrigerator. There's some kind of fungus stuff growing on them. It waved to me. GROSS!

This concludes Scab News for today. Isabelle Catherine McNally reporting.

"I don't see what a stupid stunt has to do with being president."

Why do girls have to make everything SO complicated?

"It's simple. They bring it. I eat it. They think it's a great stunt. They vote for me."

"But . . . why?"

"It'll prove I have guts," I say. "Kids like kids with guts. Kids with guts make good leaders, don't they?"

"Maybe. . . . I don't know."

"Please, Izzy, don't tattle."

"You should be writing your campaign speech, not doing dumb stunts for attention."

"So you won't tell? See, Izzy, everybody is really excited about this."

My sister sees the line of kids eagerly talking and laughing. She sees my clasped hands begging her to be on my side. For once.

Isabelle sighs. "All right. I won't tell. But if you get sick and die, don't come running to me."

CHAPTER

9

The Most Important Thing

Someone is knocking at my lab door.

"Can't you read the sign? My lab is C-L-O-S-E-D, Isabelle." I am on the floor doing sit-ups. It's part of my training. I always do a hundred sit-ups before every stunt.

Seven . . . eight . . . nine . . .

Now that I think about it, twenty sit-ups are probably plenty.

Two more sharp knocks.

"Go away, Izzy! Can't you spell? I'm in training."

Where was I? Nineteen, I think. And . . . twenty. Whew!

My door is opening.

"Geez, don't you have ears? I said—Oh, hey, Dad. If this is about what Isabelle put in her report about me, it's not true. I didn't turn all the library books in the display case at school upside down."

"You didn't?"

"No." When I see him grin, I know it is okay to confess. "I forgot one."

He chuckles. "What are you in training for?"

★ **SCAB'S TIP #9** ★

Before doing your dare-devil stunt, suspend all experiments for at least forty-eight hours. You can't do a stunt if you're grounded for figuring how much tapioca pudding it takes to fill your sister's knit Hello Kitty hat.*

*Two and two-thirds cups

"Oh—nothing. I was trying to get Izzy to stop bugging me."

My father nods and looks around at the mess. My workshop desk is covered with stuff: books, magazine articles, papers, scissors, glue sticks, duct tape, dog treats, earmuffs (don't ask). Little yellow sticky notes are plastered on my computer, on the wall, on my clock, even on my model airplanes. Some of the sticky notes have ideas for inventions. Some have ideas to fix things that are wrong with old inventions. A few have questions that I hope to find the answers to. The place may look like a tornado hit, but I know where everything is.

When I catch my dad glancing at my open inventor's notebook, I spring up. My notebook is full of top secret stuff. "So what's up?"

He turns. I slide past him and quietly shut the notebook. This is Scab's Inventor's Notebook #2. My other one is hidden behind my dresser in my blue plastic Hot Wheels collector's case. My notebooks contain all of my ideas, questions, notes, experiments, projects, inventions, and formulas. Everything is backed up on external hard drive and CD, of course.

✳ NOTES ✳

✳ Do fish sneeze?

✳ Are jelly beans made from jellyfish?

✳ Don't use Fruit Roll-Ups for edible sock invention

✳ Brocco-bot: mini robot that eats your broccoli

✳ Distance from Odor ÷ Size of Nostrils
   (−Amount of Snot in Nose) = Speed of Smell

My dad kneels down to pet Joe. My dog is taking a nap on pile number three (clean laundry I am supposed to put away, but never do). "Your mom said you didn't want to come down for dinner. You okay?"

"Uh-huh. Not hungry, that's all."

"Too many pizza rolls after school?"

"Yep," I lie. I sure can't tell him I am making room in my stomach to vacuum up tomorrow's gross-out buffet, can I?

"Did you have a good lunch today?" He is sizing me up, which has me worried that Isabelle broke her promise. She has this evil way of tattling without really tattling. She'll let you ask a bunch of questions, then nod or shake her head after each one until you guess what's on her mind. She tattles without saying a word. See what I mean? Evil.

"I sure did," I say, keeping my voice cool and calm. "Bologna, egg, marshmallow, and ketchup sandwich." My voice cracks.

"Sooooo. How's the election going?"

"It's going."

"Do you know what you're going to say in your speech?"

"Oh, yeah. You bet. Absolutely."

Haven't a clue. The most important thing is my stunt.

"You know, the most important thing, Scab," my dad says, "isn't winning. It's trying."

Trying? He's kidding, right? Nobody remembers who *tried* to win the World Series.

"So do your best. Take the high road. Be a good sport."

Does he want me to do all of these things? How about if I pick just one?

"And remember, son, no matter what happens, your mother and I will always be proud of you."

I cringe. I'm getting the No Matter What Happens speech. That's the one your parents give you when they are certain you are about to tank. Ouch.

My lab door bursts open so hard it ricochets off the little rubber stopper on the wall. "Scab, I've got the— Oh." Doyle stops short. He's holding a piece of paper. He throws his arm behind his back. Real cool. Not. "Hi, uh . . . Mr. McNally."

"Doyle." My dad stands up. "You boys wouldn't be cooking up anything, would you?"

"A new invention," I say before my best friend starts leaking secrets all over my floor. "We'll show you when we get further along, Dad."

"All right," says my dad, eyeing us. "Just don't blow up the house."

Doyle scoots past my dad, keeping his arms behind him. His face has no color. I slap him on the back. Hard. He starts breathing again.

"If you change your mind about dinner, come on down, boys. We're having Chinese chicken salad."

"Okay, Dad. Thanks."

When my dad leaves, I shut the door and shove my chair under the doorknob. "What have we got?"

Doyle hands me the sign-up sheet.

"This isn't so bad," I say, looking over the list of food I'm going to be horking down tomorrow. "I can

WHAT DO *YOU* WANT TO SEE
★ SCAB EAT? ★

★ Cloey — boiled liver and onions

★ Meggie — pickled herring jam

★ Juan — stinky cheese

★ Beth — sardines

★ Elliot — creamed cabbage

★ Alec — my mom's steamed prune pudding

★ Kinsey — lemon

★ Lewis — gooey pumpkin guts and dirt

★ Henry — fried squid

★ Felicia — lime Jell-O with nuts & tuna

★ Jordyn — garlic

★ Carlton — fossilized fruitcake

do these. What is it with Lewis and dirt?"

"Ignore it. I crossed it out," says Doyle. "The best part is, you only have to eat one bite of each thing."

"No problem. Easiest daredevil stunt ever."

Doyle flops onto my bed. "I talked to Will. He's going to keep Mrs. Zaff busy so she won't get in our way."

"He is? How?"

"Pop out his trick shoulder."

"Good. It's creepier than the knee."

"I was thinking we'd set up at table four—"

"Where's Never Missy's food?" I ask, scanning the list a second time.

"She didn't sign up to bring anything."

"Nothing?"

"Nope."

"That's weird."

"Nah, she's scared. She knows she's going down. You're going to smoke her in the election and there's nothing she can do about it. It's over. I'll bet she doesn't even come to school tomorrow. Anyway, as I was saying, I'm going to set you up at table four. It's right in the middle of the row where everybody can see you . . ."

As Doyle talks, I can't help but wonder what Never Missy is up to. It's not like her to give up so easily. On the other hand, she *was* pretty steamed at me today. Could Doyle be right? Has Never Missy decided to give up? She's never lost before. It's tough to lose. I ought to know—I do it once a week. Sometimes twice.

I lie down beside Joe on the pile of clean clothes. I don't feel so good. I'm not hungry. I'm not sick. But I'm not well, either. I don't know what's wrong.

Nerves, I bet. I take a deep breath and listen to my best friend talk about the stunt. I'm glad he's here, because I can't shake the feeling that a bunch of slimy green tentacles are out there.

Somewhere.

Waiting to strike.

10

Showtime

Have a nice day. Have a nice day. Good luck with the stunt, Scab."

A second away from hopping off the bus, I swing my head around. Zombie eyes are staring into mine.

The corners of Ms. Rigormortis's mouth inch upward. Was that a smile? Before I can decide, the lips are a straight line once again. "Have a nice day. Have a nice day."

I hop off the bus. Doyle meets me at the curb. We walk to class in silence. There is nothing to say. He knows what he needs to do. I know what I need to do. I am so focused, it takes me a few minutes after the bell rings to realize the desk in front of me is empty. I can see into the shelf. There are several blue pens, the red puffball pen, a heart-shaped eraser, and a couple of those dumb yellow paper umbrellas. A see-through purple plastic ruler is teetering on the edge of a pencil holder. It looks like Never Missy is going to be tardy. Miss Sweetandsour takes roll after the bell. About twenty minutes into our geography lesson I realize Never Missy isn't tardy. She isn't coming at all! How about that? Doyle was right. She *is* scared of me. She's given up. I've won! Scab McNally, Class President. I should print it on a T-shirt or something.

"My dad boiled up a fresh batch of liver last night," Cloey whispers into my ear.

I figured. I could smell her from the parking lot. I turn around. Cloey is wearing a white V-neck sweater with three giant sunflowers sewn on the front. The yellow petals stick out in 3-D.

"I'm ready," I say. "If I eat the liver, you're going to vote for me, right?"

She bites her lip. "Ummmmm."

"Come on, Cloey."

She touches the brown center of one of the 3-D sunflowers. "If you eat a bite of *everything*, I guess I could vote for you."

"Swear?"

She bends her pinky. I forgot. Girls pinky swear. Guys spit swear. It think it means more when you hurl saliva, but what can you do? I hook my pinky around hers and we shake on it.

I look at Never Missy's chair. There's a crack in the seat. I know it's dumb, but I am starting to feel sorry for her. Kind of. I wanted to beat her, sure, but

SCAB'S SECRET TO SUCCESSFUL
✷ SPIT SWEARING ✷

PUT YOUR LIPS TOGETHER LIKE YOU'RE GOING to suck a really thick milk shake through a straw. Suck in as much air as you can. Gather up all the spit at the back of your throat, aim at your target, and then blow with everything you've got. Spit missile!

I never meant to frighten her away. What if she never comes back to school? I decide that, since I am almost president, I won't be mad at Never Missy anymore for snagging my glow-in-the-dark rat. I lean forward and push the tippy purple ruler back into her desk.

It's nearly lunchtime when Miss Sweetandsour looks around the room. "You've all been so quiet this morning. Who are you and what have you done with my class?"

"We're hungry," I say, rubbing my stomach. "I sure hope there's something good for lunch today."

Everybody laughs. Our teacher looks confused.

When the bell rings, we race for the cafeteria. On the way, Will gives me a slap on the back. "Go get 'em," he says, rotating his shoulder. "I wish I could see it."

"Thanks for keeping me from getting Zaffed."

"Any time. Good luck."

We knock knuckles.

"Come on, Scab," says Doyle. "Do you have enough water? How are you feeling? Should you eat something first? I brought some crackers—"

I give him my best lion roar. "Let's do this!"

Doyle goes into the cafeteria ahead of me. "Make room for Scab! Clear the way for the Human Vacuum!"

As I pass, kids start clapping and yelling.

"Go, Scab!"

"You can do it!"

Supreme sweetness! I punch the air above my head. This is going to be my greatest stunt ever. My heart is slamming against my chest. I take a few deep breaths. I hop from one foot to the other while Doyle lines up everybody's food on table four. Now is the time to use my "don't" strategy. Don't think. Don't smell. Don't taste. The idea is to chew once (twice tops), swallow, and keep moving. When Doyle is through, he nods for me to step up to the first container. Whew! My eyes fill with water. Instantly, I know what this is: Cloey's liver and onions. Doyle hands me a bottle of water. I twist off the cap.

"Quiet!" my best friend shouts to the crowd. "The Human Vacuum needs absolute silence. We're about to start."

Everyone hushes up. They huddle in. I search their faces. I don't see Isabelle. I hope she isn't in the main office tattling. I feel warm. And a little dizzy.

Doyle looks at me. "One bite, remember?"

"Right." I gulp. The key to a successful stunt is mind over matter. If I believe I can do it, I *will* do it. Your body naturally follows your brain. Simple as that. I wiggle my fingers. They feel funny. Tingly.

"I'll give you the signal," says Doyle. There is no time limit, but we both know the faster I go, the sooner I finish. "Ready?"

I take a swig of water. I glance around. Still no Isabelle. "Ready."

"Set."

I reach for the plastic fork. I am inches from stabbing Cloey's liver and onions—

"Wait!"

The crowd moans.

"You down there," Doyle calls, peering down the table. A couple of third graders are leaning over the last plastic container. "Get back. In fact, everybody, take one step backward. Give the Human Vacuum some room."

Murmuring, the kids do what he says. I'm glad. My T-shirt is sticking to my back. My feet are broiling. My fingertips are frostbitten.

"What about a barf bag?" That's Cloey.

"Got one," answers Doyle. He pulls a dark green trash bag from under the table. He nudges me and grins. "We're not going to need it, though, are we?"

"Nope."

Doyle raises his hand for quiet, and the chatter dies down. "Ready, Scab?"

I take two big breaths. I shake out my icy hands and remind myself this is all about brain over body. Mind. Over. Matter. I pick up the fork. I give my best friend a nod.

"Set."

Mind over matter. Mind over matter.

"GO!"

The next minute of my life is a blur of screaming kids, weird smells, and even weirder tastes. It goes something like this:

Slithery, soupy gel.

Water.

Fishy slime with a sugary aftertaste.

More water.

Whoa! *That* is stinky cheese. Stuck in throat. Help!

Water. Water. *Water.*

Something with a fish head. Was that an eyeball?

"Eat it, Scab!"

"You can do it!" The chanting sounds miles away.

Gloppy leaves in sour milk.

Squishy, chewy blobs. Burned pie crust.

Water.

Za-zing! Lemon!

Stringy, stinky orange mess. Raw pumpkin goo is the worst. Lewis is a toad.

Water. Water.

"Eat, eat, eat!"

Crispy—no wait, slippery.

Slithery fish wrapped in crunchy.

Ka-chunk! Ech—bitter. My eyes sting. Garlic, of course.

Ouch! My tooth hits something hard. Gravel?

I open my eyes wider to see a rust-brown rectangle stuffed with red and green chunks. Carlton's fruitcake. Wow, it *is* old. That's when it hits me. I am at the final plastic container. I'm finished!

Doyle throws my arm into the air. "The Human Vacuum has done it!"

My class cheers. Henry bangs his shoulder into mine. Alec shakes my hand. Other kids push in to ruffle my hair and congratulate me. I feel like a rock star.

"Good job, Scab," says Cloey. "Are you all right?"

I am still working on Carlton's fossilized fruitcake, so the best I can do is pat my stomach and give her a thumbs-up.

"Vote Scab," cries Doyle as kids leave. "Don't forget to vote Scab for president this afternoon. You're voting for Scab, aren't you, Cloey?"

"You bet—"

"Stop!"

I scan the cafeteria for Mrs. Zaff or Mr. Huckabee, the principal, but don't see any—

Wuh-oh.

A purple blob is coming this way. For the first time today, my stomach tightens.

"I have something for the Human Vacuum!" shouts Never Missy, pushing against the tide of kids.

Doyle steps in to block her. "You're too late."

"He's right. It's all over," says Cloey, smoothing down a sunflower on her sweater.

"Scab's finished," says Doyle, trying to shoo her away.

Gasping, she looks at them. Then she looks at me. "So you won't do it? You won't eat what I brought?" Her voice sounds funny. Her *r*'s sound like *w*'s. Her cheeks are puffy. And pink. Never Missy is sick.

"Sorry," I say, though I'm really not.

"Some daredevil you are." She unzips her coat.

I jump back. I figure this is it. Eight (or more) slimy green tentacles are going to shoot out, grab me, and hurl me across the room. But that's not what happens. Instead, Never Missy takes a sandwich bag out of her inside pocket. She holds it up. I see a bunch of tiny, wrinkled, red tomatoes inside.

"See? They're not so bad," she lisps. "They're kind of cute, I think. I'll even eat one first, if you want."

"Didn't you hear me? The stunt is over," says Doyle firmly.

"Fine," says Never Missy. "I'll just tell our class that you guys lied."

"Have you flipped your gourd?" asks my best friend. "Nobody lied."

"You said the Human Vacuum could eat anything."

"You were supposed to sign up like everybody else *and* you were supposed to get here on time," he snaps. "And what's with the Daffy Duck impression anyway?"

"It's okay, Doyle," I say. "I'm not afraid of your tomatoes, Missy. I'll eat them."

"That's better," she says, though it comes out. "Thath betta."

"The stunt's not over!" Lewis shouts, cupping his hands around his mouth. "Come back, everybody. Scab's going to eat more stuff. Come back!"

"Scab," Doyle hisses. "You've already got enough votes to win the election. You don't have to prove anything to anyone, especially her. . . ."

But he's talking to himself. My eyes are locked onto Never Missy's. And hers onto mine. She sits down at table four with a carton of milk and her sandwich bag. I take the seat across from her. I do not blink. Neither does she. Kids cluster around us. Now that most everyone in the cafeteria has finished eating, the crowd is even bigger than it was during my original stunt. Okay by me. I can eat anything, anytime, in front of anyone. Mind over matter, right?

Never Missy opens the bag. Gently, she takes out one of the miniature tomatoes. She holds it by its little green stem. I do not blink. She smiles at me. I do not smile back. Never Missy pops the thing in her mouth. She chews several times then swallows. I watch her face. Her gray eyes get a little teary, but that's it. No squished-up nose. No puckered mouth. No horrible scream. Never Missy reaches for her milk and takes a long drink. "Easy," she says, her voice a bit hoarse. She slides the bag toward me. "Easy as can be."

I gulp some water. I reach into the bag. I take out the teeniest, wrinkliest tomato I can find. I hold it by its stem so I can get a good look at—

Isabelle! My sister is standing directly behind Never Missy. Isabelle is slowly shaking her head. Her mouth is forming a word. *Noooooo.*

Never Missy sighs. "You going to eat it, Scab, or talk to it?"

I open my mouth. My sister covers her eyes. I place the shriveled tomato on my tongue. A second after I sink my teeth into it I know I have made a mistake. My tongue, my throat, my nostrils—everything from the neck up starts to burn.

Fire! My entire face is on fire. I've never felt pain like this before, not even when I shut the car door on my thumb when I was six. I can't talk. I can't yell. Has my tongue fallen out yet? I am sure it is nothing but a charred black blob. I am gagging. Doyle starts pounding my back. He hits me so hard the tomato flies out of my mouth. Thank goodness. I chug water from my bottle, but can't put out the flames.

"Owwwwww!" Forget my mind. My matter is screaming. And so is someone else.

"Ewwwww!" I hear the shriek a second before Cloey races past the table. That's when I spot my half-chewed tomato. It's stuck to the middle of a 3-D sunflower on the front of Cloey's sweater. "Get it off!" she shouts. "Somebody get Scab's spewage off me!"

CHAPTER

11

Same Old Chair,
Same Old Place

Back and forth. Back and forth. I swing my legs. Back and forth.

I make sure not to kick anything, flick anything, or lick anything. Mrs. Lipwart, the school secretary, has got her eye on me. The pink knobby thing growing out of her top lip is watching me, too. It's about the size of our TV satellite dish. When she gets mad, the knobby thing turns red. When she gets really mad, it starts throbbing. You do not want to be around when that happens.

I am sitting outside the principal's office in my favorite chair. It's next to the white plastic table in the corner with the big cactus and a stack of magazines. I'm holding a pink detention slip. Thank you, Mrs. Zaff and Cloey, the girl with the colossal lungs. I rip the corners off the slip so it looks like a stop sign.

Lunch recess is almost over. I will probably be stuck here waiting for the principal for most of the afternoon. At least I won't have to be in Room 242 when Never Missy wins the election. I rip a photo of a woman in a long dress out of one of the magazines—well, most of her. I leave her head. I am about to stick the headless girl onto the front of the cactus when I hear, "Pssst!"

It's Doyle. He's outside in the hall. Nobody is supposed to be in the building during lunch recess. If Mrs. Lipwart catches him, he'll get one of these little slips for himself.

"Your ears are glowing," he whispers.

"My tongue hurts. It feels like I ate a stingy jellyfish instead of a tomato."

"That was no tomato. That was a chili pepper."

"A pepper?"

"Yep. It's called a Red Savina. Isabelle says it's one of the hottest chili peppers in the world."

"No kidding?" I perk up. "Sweet! I, Scab McNally, the Human Vacuum, ate one of the hottest chili peppers in the world."

"Noooooo," says my best friend. "You, Scab McNally, the Human Vacuum, *spit out* one of the hottest chili peppers in the world onto the new sweater of one of the loudest girls in the world."

Oh, yeah. I tip my chair back until my head hits the wall. "Is Cloey all right?"

"Yep. Your sister is helping her wash off her sweater."

"I can't figure it out. Never Missy ate that hot pepper like it was candy."

"Must be an alien thing," says Doyle.

"It isn't good, is it?"

Doyle lifts a shoulder. He doesn't want to say what we both already know. That's the problem with daredevil stunts. If you succeed, you're a hero. If you don't, well . . . you can forget about becoming class president anytime this century.

"Treasurer is still open," Doyle says meekly.

I groan.

"Mr. Ferguson!"

Bug spit! We've been caught by the Wart.

I move like lightning to get my chair on all four legs.

"I'm scramming, Mrs. L.!" shouts Doyle.

We knock knuckles and he takes off.

I finish pinning the headless girl to the cactus. I give her a chocolate cupcake to hold that is three times bigger than she is. I also give her Brad Pitt's head. I go through the whole stack of magazines. No sports. No comics. No reptiles. You'd think Mrs. Lipwart would have something here for me. After all, I spend more time in this chair than anybody. A piece of paper falls out of one of the magazines. Aw, geez. It's Never Missy's handout. I start to make it into a paper airplane, but I can't help myself. I read it.

If you ignore all those dumb happy faces, some of Never Missy's ideas really aren't so bad. Wouldn't you know it? Bug spit!

★ NEVER MISSY'S HANDOUT ★

GREETINGS! I AM MISSY MAL☺NE AND I WANT TO be Y☺UR next class president. Why do I want to be Y☺UR president? I would like to make our classroom better. In fact, I would like to make our whole school better. How will I do this? Here are some of the things I want to accomplish as Y☺UR president:

- ☺ Update our fourth-grade web page.
- ☺ Get more students to volunteer for math tutoring club. (The younger kids need our help!)
- ☺ Organize a fundraiser (with the PTA) to buy new flowers for the courtyard.
- ☺ Bring more guest speakers to our class, especially authors and artists!
- ☺ Make sure none of our playground equipment is missing or broken. (I hate flat four-square balls.)
- ☺ Get rid of the weird, green, chunky salad dressing in the cafeteria once and for all.

By the way, I was treasurer last year in Mrs. Lange's class and I never missed a *single* student council meeting. I also went to leadership camp last summer. So please vote for ME, Missy Mal☺ne, and I will work super hard for Y☺U!

I go back to folding Never Missy's handout into a paper airplane. I wait for Mrs. Lipwart to go into the nurse's office before I launch the plane. It flies across the check-in desk and does one loop before smashing into the bulletin board. The plane drops onto Mrs. Lipwart's desk. Oops. When she comes back I am lying on my back across the row of chairs. My eyes are closed.

"Nice plane, Mr. McNally," I hear. "I'm sure Mr. Huckabee will enjoy it as much as I do."

I let out a little snore. I guess I take a real nap because when I open my eyes Never Missy is standing over me. Her hair is almost touching my chin.

"You alive?" Never Missy's voice sounds a little more normal.

I quickly sit up. She is holding out a carton of milk with a straw in it.

"What is it—poison?"

"It will help with the burning."

"Burning? What burning. I feel great."

She sits down next to me. I want to move over,

but then I'd be sitting on the cactus. I'm stuck here in this corner. For now.

Never Missy whistles. "I've never seen anybody's face get *that* red *that* fast."

I adjust Brad Pitt's head.

She clears her throat. "Sorry about the peppers, Scab. I didn't realize they were superspicy hot. I've never eaten one before either. My mom buys them

at the farmer's market downtown to make her chili at our restaurant. She calls it her five-alarm chili. Get it? It's so hot, like a five-alarm fire?"

"Yeah, I get it." I didn't know Never Missy's family owned a restaurant.

"I *am* sorry," she says quietly—not at all the way she says it when we play Fly Around the World. I glance at her. Never Missy's gray eyes are soft and watery. When she holds out the milk again, I take it. I sip a little, then wait and sip some more. She is right. It cools my aching taste buds.

I start to ask. "So how did you—?"

"Miss Malone!" The Wart again.

Never Missy pops to her feet.

"Don't you have something for me?"

"My excuse." Never Missy puts her hands to her puffy cheeks. "I forgot."

"You were supposed to check in immediately when you got back from the dentist."

"I know. I'm sorry. I have a note from my mom." Never Missy scurries up to the desk.

I look at the principal's door. Is Mr. Huckabee ever coming out? Maybe he's not even in today. I wonder if I should check—

Dentist?

The word echoes in my head.

So that's where Never Missy was all morning. She didn't drop out of school. She went to get her teeth cleaned or get a filling or something. It must have been a filling, because she was talking funny at lunch.

"Oh, man!" I shout out loud. Everything makes sense now. Never Missy ate that hot pepper so easily because she couldn't taste it. *Her mouth was numb!*

What a great stunt!

Bug spit!

That is a good trick. I wish I had thought of it.

When Never Missy comes back, she has a shy grin. She knows I know. I wonder why Mrs. Lipwart doesn't make her leave the office, but I don't ask. Never Missy sits down next to me. She unbuttons her coat. I sneak a look. I see a white shirt with blue buttons tucked into a pair of jeans. I see a long silver chain with a turquoise giraffe. Not a slimy green tentacle in sight. I have to admit, I'm a little disappointed.

Mr. Huckabee's door opens. His shiny bald head appears. "Scab, come on in." He sighs. The principal's sighs are getting longer as the semester goes on.

Never Missy stands up. She heads for Mr. Huckabee's office.

I tap her shoulder. "Where are you going?"

"Where do you think?"

The bell rings.

Two dimples appear on each side of her face. "It's only fair."

CHAPTER

12

A Few Election Surprises

Never Missy and I walk into Room 242 twelve minutes after the bell rings. Our class has already started afternoon silent reading. When everyone sees us, they start whispering.

"Eyes on your books and mouths closed, please," says Miss Sweetandsour. She holds her hand out for Never Missy's hall pass. I wait my turn. I can see Doyle out of the corner of my eye. He's got a big book with a Komodo dragon on the cover. He's leaning as far as he can out the side of his desk, trying to get my attention. Doyle wants to know what happened in the principal's office. He wants to know what in the world I am doing with the enemy. Later, I will explain that I got two days of after-school detention for my stunt. It probably would have been more if Never Missy hadn't said what she'd said to Mr. Huckabee.

"It's my fault too," she said. "Scab did the stunt, but I made it worse. Whatever you give Scab, Mr. Huckabee, you should give to me, too."

Never Missy got her wish. She told me afterward that it was her first after-school detention ever, but she didn't sound mad.

I just realized my leg is twitching. It's not the detention. Detention I'm used to. What's bugging me is that I think I am starting to like Never Missy. I hate that I am starting to like Never Missy.

"Miss Sweeten?" I ask.

"Yes?"

Then I say what I knew I'd say the minute Never Missy walked into the principal's office two steps ahead of me. "I don't want to run for president anymore."

Her eyebrows hit her hairline. "You don't?"

THINGS TO DO IN DETENTION
(BESIDES YOUR HOMEWORK)

☑ Connect your arm freckles with a pen. Mine make a chicken.

☑ Count the teeny holes in the ceiling tiles (there are 14,307 in our detention room—wait, 14,308—shoot, let me get back to you on that).

☑ Make a replica of Mrs. Lipwart's lip wart using the gum on the bottom of your desk.

☑ Get the attention of a girl on the other side of the room. Rub your face like you're trying to tell her she's got something on *her* face. Then keep shaking your head when she tries to wipe it off.

I shake my head.

"Is something wrong, Scab?"

"No . . . it's just that . . ." I don't know how to explain it to her so she will understand. I don't want her to think I am a quitter. "Remember when you said that we shouldn't try to buy votes from people? That we should try to earn them?"

"Yes."

"Nev—I mean, Missy . . . well, she sort of . . . I guess she . . . she earned my vote. Know what I mean?" I don't want to look at her, but I do want to look at her. So I take a chance. I look.

My teacher is . . .

. . . smiling. Miss Sweetandsour's green eyes are all soft and crinkly. And they are looking right at me. At *me*! I can think of only one thing to do. I smile back. It's better than I ever imagined.

When the final bell rings at 3:12 p.m., kids run for the buses. I don't run anywhere. My stomach is making odd noises. My throat is sore. My tongue throbs. I may stay home tomorrow. Call it a stunt recovery day. I zip up my backpack and heave it onto my shoulder. It feels twice as heavy as it usually does.

"Scab," Miss Sweeten calls as I shuffle past. "Will you stop by the staff room and take home your dead artwork?

"Sure."

"Mrs. Lippman will let you in."

"Did I get an A?"

"Will you take it home *today*?"

"Uh-huh."

"You got an A."

Sweet! I walk out the door and bump smack into Isabelle.

"How'd it go?" she asks.

"I'm not class president."

"Awwwwww." She puts an arm around my shoulders. "How are you holding up?"

"I'm okay," I say, but my sister isn't listening. She starts walking me down the hall like she is the mom and I am the three-year-old who did a face plant off the seesaw.

"That's too bad, Scab. But you've got to put more effort into it if you want to win."

"I know."

"You can't have a lazy attitude."

"I know."

"You've got to take every vote seriously."

"I know."

"If people think you don't care, they won't elect you—"

"Oh, I got elected, all right."

★ DID YOU EVER WONDER... ★

WHO CAME UP WITH THE FREAKY SCHOOL TIME schedule? Our first recess starts at 10:07 a.m., lunch ends at 12:33 p.m., and school lets out at 3:12 p.m. Doyle says teachers do this to mess with our heads.

"But you said—"

"I didn't get elected *president*."

"What?"

I throw my arms open wide. "I got elected treasurer."

She gulps. "Treasurer?"

"He's going to regret it," says Cloey, sailing past us.

I laugh. I'm not worried. I can handle the job. After all, I ate one of the hottest peppers on Earth and I'm still here, right?

"Mooooooooom," cries Cloey, "look what Scab did to my sweater!"

I decide it's a good time to escape. "Meet you on

the bus, Izzy. I have to pick up my dead art." I spin on my heels. I wonder if I am the first student to ever see inside the faculty room. I wonder if it's as big as I've pictured it—the Teacher Torture Board, I mean.

I hear my sister calling after me. "Dead art?"

CHAPTER
13

It's Friday. Again. Ugh.

Scab, please remove the paperclips from your earlobes," says Miss Sweetandsour. "You know what to do."

I know what to do, all right. I just don't want to do it.

I sigh. I have no choice but to obey my teacher. I pull three small paperclips off my right earlobe and four off my left. I get to my feet. I stand to the left of my desk. Never Missy stands to the right. We are playing Fly Around the World. Again. Never Missy has already beaten me once today and is back to whip my butt again.

Leaning back, I find Doyle across the room.

He raises his fist. *Don't give up.*

I raise mine. *I won't.*

Doyle says even though I blew the stunt, I would have won the election anyway. Maybe. Maybe not. He says I ought to run for class president again next year. I might. If I do, it'll be because I want the job. I think I'll see how being treasurer goes first.

"Scab? Missy?" Miss Sweetandsour straightens her deck of flash cards. "Are you ready?"

Missy flips her bangs out of her eyes. "Ready," she says.

"Ready," I say.

My heart picks up speed. My mouth is dry. I wipe my hands on the sides of my jeans. Why do I always get so nervous? This time I am going to beat her. I know, I know, I say it every Friday afternoon, but today—

The card comes up.

I see white. And a division sign. Sixty-three divided by seven is—

"Nine!"

"Correct," says Miss Sweetandsour.

My head drops.

The class starts clapping and stomping their feet. Wait a second. Was that—?

Did I—?

Yes! That *was* me. I have done it. I have beat the unbeatable Never Missy Malone.

"Wahoo!" shouts Will. "Way to go, Scab."

Cloey pounds her palms on her desk. Doyle's shrill whistle floats across the room.

Miss Sweetandsour is writing my name on her notepad. I can see her making the letters. *S-C-A-B*. She has never written my name on *that* pad before. I usually get the pink one. It feels good.

I glance at Never Missy.

She pulls her arms up into her purple jacket. "You can say it."

Oh, yeah! *Vroom, vroom sorry. Vroom, vroom, sor-reeeeee.*

The words have been festering like an infected splinter under my thumbnail. Finally, it's my chance to shout them out the way Never Missy always does. I want to. But for some reason, I don't. I can't say why. I just don't.

Never Missy slides into my seat. It's weird to see her sitting there, in my desk, twirling one of her alien antennae. Weird in a good way.

I don't move. Not a muscle. I am waiting, waiting, waiting . . .

"Scab," Miss Sweetandsour says gently, her lips curving upward, "you may fly on."

TRUDI TRUEIT knew she'd found her life's passion after writing (and directing) her first play in fourth grade. Since then, she's been a newspaper journalist, television news reporter/anchor, media specialist, and freelance writer, and is now a children's book author. She has published more than forty fiction and non-fiction titles for young readers. Trudi drew inspiration for SECRETS OF A LAB RAT from her experiences growing up with her little brother, who also fancied himself a daredevil, and somehow survived childhood despite his many stunts.

truditrueit.com

JIM PAILLOT lives in Arizona with his wife, Lisa, and two children. They have dogs, hamsters, and a lizard. When Jim is not drawing, he is usually hiking, reading, or swimming with his kids. They collect old tin robots, watch cartoons, and travel as much as possible. Once when Jim was a kid, an anchor fell on his head. Strange but true!

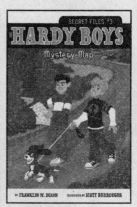